BUBBIE'S
MAGICAL
HAIR
Written by Abbe Rolnick
Illustrated by Lynda Porter

WHEN THE WARM
WIND RUSTLES
WITH A HINT OF LAUGHTER

BUBBIE GLIDES IN WITH HER MAGICAL HAIR.

LONG STRANDS
THAT TICKLE

WHEN SHE TWIRLS YOU AROUND,

BUBBIE'S HAIR RISES AND FALLS

AS IT SWEEPS
DUST BUNNIES
UNDER THE BED.

BROWN CURLS TURNED TO GRAY WAVES...

BUBBIE WINDS HER HAIR THROUGH
THE TALES SHE HAS LIVED.

BUBBIE'S MAGICAL HAIR
TRANSFORMS LAUGHTER

INTO A
WILLOW TREE...

THAT SWAYS AS SHE UNLEASHES

HER SILVER LOCKS WITHIN ITS BRANCHES.

BUBBIE'S HAIR SMELLS
OF BAKED STRUDEL

AND DUNKING COOKIES FILLED WITH HOMEMADE JAM!

WHEN BUBBIE WASHES HER HAIR
IN YOUR TEARS

RIVERS FLOW.

BUBBIE'S MAGICAL HAIR SHIMMERS

THROUGH THE SEASONS OF TIME.

THE GREEN OF LEAVES,
BROWN OF DIRT, BLUE OF SKY.

AND WHITE OF SNOW,
SCATTER AS SHE SHAKES HER HEAD.

STOP
THOUGHTS
REALIGN...

NOW PUFFED
WITH PURPOSE.

BUBBIE CUTS
HER LONG LOCKS,
AS BUBBIES DO

THE WORLD PAUSES
AS THE CURLS FALL.

ALL IS BREATHLESS UNTIL
THE SILVER ENDS GROW WITH NEW LIFE:

RIBBONS, STARS, AND
DANDELION DUST SPREAD MAGIC.

BUBBIE HAS MANY NAMES.

GRANDMA & GRAMMY

LOOK FOR HER
IN THE MIRROR,
IN THE POCKET
OF YOUR COAT, AND
WHEN YOU LOOK BOTH WAYS
CROSSING THE STREET.

YOU'LL FIND BUBBIE'S MAGIC IN THE GRASS.

IN THE WISPS OF CLOUDS, AND IN THE STARS.

FEEL BUBBIE'S MAGIC IN YOUR HEART.

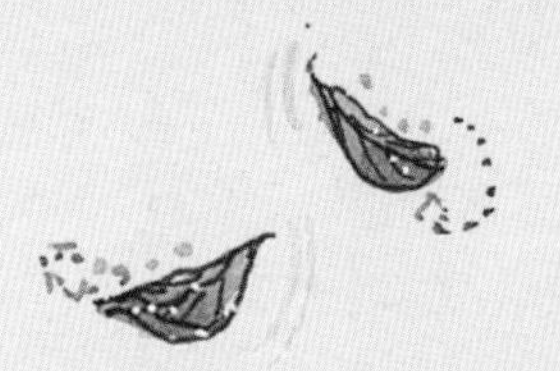

DEDICATION

TO MY GRANDCHILDREN WHO INSPIRED THIS BOOK,
PAIGE AND LANE PORTER, AND TO ALL MY FUTURE GRANDCHILDREN.
MOST ESPECIALLY TO MY OWN BUBBIE, MARY JAVODICK,
WHO SHOWED ME WONDER AND GRACE.

BUBBIE'S MAGICAL HAIR

Design & Prepress by Sally Dunn Design and Photography, www.sallysuedunn.com
Copy Editor by Nevin Mays Editorial, www.nevinmays.com
Library of Congress Control Number: 2020921759 Rolnick, Abbe
ISBN: 978-0-9995291-9-5 (Hardback) ISBN: 978-1-7360878-0-0 (Electronic)

Other books by Abbe Rolnick:
River of Angels, 2nd edition, Book One in Generations of Secrets (2018)
Color of Lies, Book Two in Generations of Secrets (2018)
Founding Stones, Book Three in Generations of Secrets (2020)
Cocoon of Cancer: An Invitation to Love Deeply (2016)
Tattle Tales: Essays and Stories Along the Way (2016)

ABBE ROLNICK grew up in the suburbs of Baltimore, Maryland. Her first major cultural jolt occurred at age 15 when her family moved to Miami Beach, Florida. After attending Boston University, she lived in Puerto Rico, where she owned a bookstore. Her writings include: *River of Angels, Color of Lies, and Founding Stones novels in the Generation of Secrets Series,* as well as C*ocoon of Cancer: An Invitation to Love Deeply, and Tattle Tales: Essays and Stories Along the Way.* Abbe lives with her husband Jim, amid twenty acres in Skagit Valley, Washington.
Visit her website, www.abberolnick.com.

Lynda Porter, raised in Ohio by an artistic family, became an art and music teacher for special needs students. She has traveled extensively with her family, living in Belgium and England. In retirement, Lynda continues to paint and travel. She resides with her husband in Anacortes, WA. Illustrator of five children's books, she authored a biography of her father's World War II experiences, which includes his paintings and hand drawn maps.

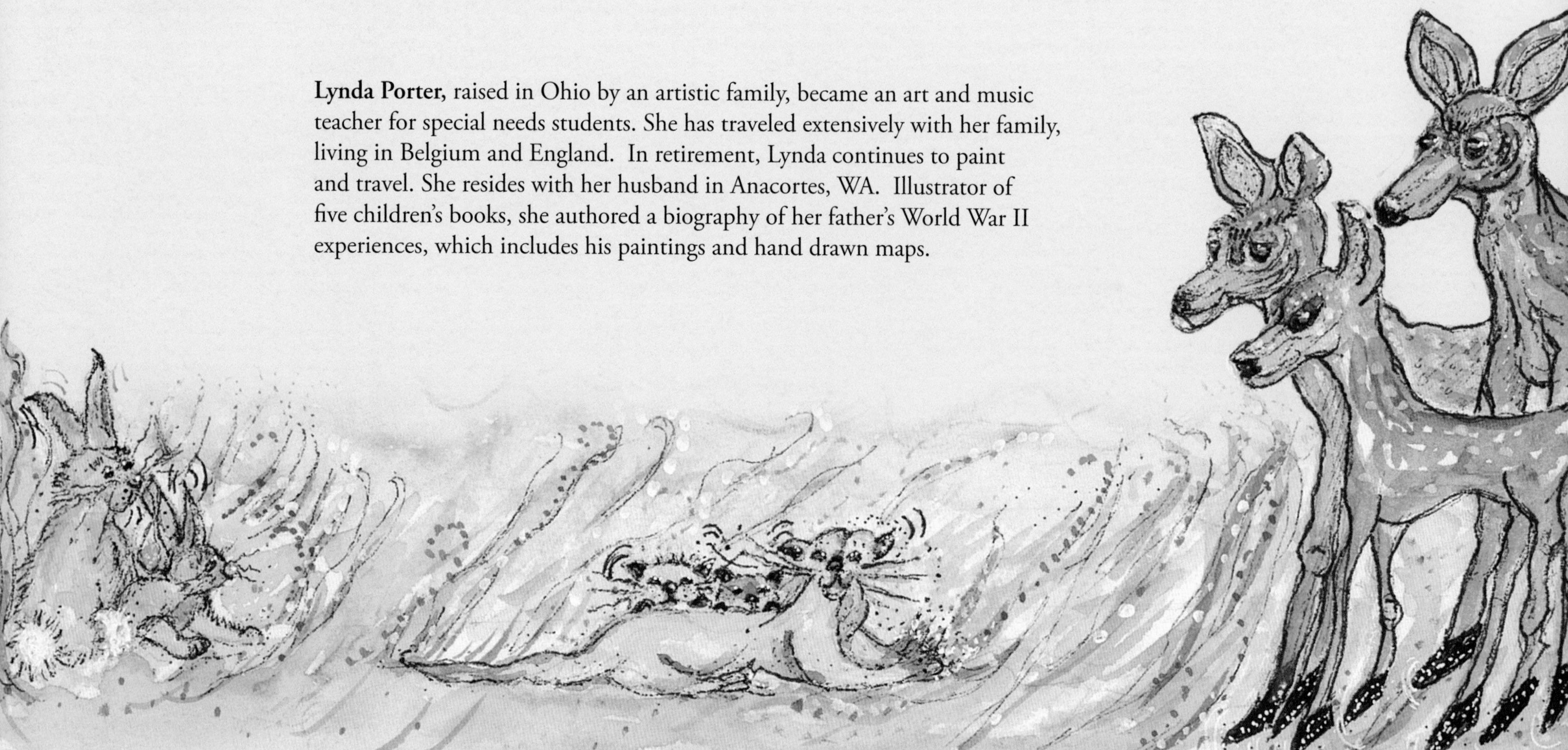